THIS BOOK
Belongs to

〰〰〰〰〰〰〰

For information address Disney Press, 1101 Flower Street,
Glendale, California 91201.

ISBN 978-1-4847-9977-2

FAC-038091-17244

Printed in the United States of America

Library of Congress Control Number: 2017942472

First Hardcover Edition, October 2017

1 3 5 7 9 10 8 6 4 2

For more Disney Press fun, visit www.disneybooks.com

I Am Not Angry!

WRITTEN BY
Marie Eden

ILLUSTRATED BY
Amy Mebberson

DISNEP PRESS

LOS ANGELES • NEW YORK

Oh, boy.

Here we go again.

I **hate** that helmet!
It pinches our ears!

Seriously.
Doesn't Mom know it gives
us major helmet hair?

Ugh!

But it's so **pretty**!

Don't you like all the
hearts and flowers?

And look!
There are rainbows!
Which come from rain!
Don't you love rainy days?

It's raining?

It's not safe to ride our bike in the rain! We could slip on the hills. And there are cracks in the sidewalk!

Oh, no. No, no, no!

We are not going out in the rain!

It's **not** raining, you **nitwit!**

This guy!

He thinks everything is out to get us. Last week it was pigeons. The week before it was Riley's pillow.

Her pillow!

What's scary about a pillow?

What's wrong with *you?*

Angry?

Of course I'm

angry.

Look at what I'm dealing with here!

What do you mean, I need to **calm down**?

This **is** me being calm!

I AM
CALM!

Um, Anger?
Are you okay?

I think I'm fine, but **someone** keeps telling me to **calm down**.

A good cry usually makes
me feel better. I find
it helps to lie on the floor.

Maybe you should give
that a try.

Is she **serious**?

Fine.

I'll give it a shot.

This is ridiculous.
I'm getting up.

Ugh.

What are you doing lying on the dirty floor?

We're trying to help Anger
calm down. **Shhh.**
Nice, deep breaths . . .

You know that's not going to work, **right**?

Okay, smarty-pants. How do
you calm down?

Actually . . . I have a
memory that always
makes me feel better.

Come on!

I'll show you.

Look at that.
Picture day at school, and we looked **perfect**!

I bet you feel better now!

Better?

Why would this make me feel **better**?

Is she **kidding?**

I have a thousand things to do
and **she** has me looking back
at **picture day**?

What are you yelling about, Anger? You know, you really need to **calm down**.

You should do what *I* do
when *I* need to calm down.

Ice-skate with Riley!
Come on!

Ice-skating?
That's her bright idea?

I feel stupid.

Are we **done** with this yet?

Oh, **you** have an idea.
This ought to be **good**.

What do I have to do?

Clench my fists and
pull up my shoulders,
then let out a
loud scream?
That actually sounds like
fun!

Okay, here goes. . . .

Hey, thanks!

I should have known that would work. Yelling always makes me feel better. We should have started with that! But you may want to go check on **Fear**.